Gobo and the River

By Joseph Killorin Brennan
Pictures by Diane Dawson Hearn

Muppet Press
Holt, Rinehart and Winston
NEW YORK

Copyright © 1985 by Henson Associates, Inc.
Fraggle Rock, Fraggles, Muppets, and character names are trademarks of Henson Associates, Inc.
All rights reserved, including the right to reproduce this
book or portions thereof in any form.
Published by Holt, Rinehart and Winston,
383 Madison Avenue, New York, New York 10017.

Library of Congress Cataloging in Publication Data
Brennan, Joseph Killorin.
Gobo and the river.
Summary: While trying to rescue Wembley when he falls
in the river, Gobo accidentally knocks himself out and
floats away to distant places he's never seen before.
1. Children's stories, American. [1. Friendship—
Fiction. 2. Rivers—Fiction. 3. Puppets—Fiction]
I. Hearn, Diane Dawson, ill. II. Title.
PZ7.B75162Go 1985 [E] 84-22369
ISBN: 0-03-004552-5

First Edition
Printed in the United States of America
1 3 5 7 9 10 8 6 4 2

ISBN 0-03-004552-5

Contents

Come Said the River

SOME days in Fraggle Rock are good for singing. Some are perfect for exploring. And every so often there comes a perfect picnic day. Today was that sort of day.

Fraggles throughout the Rock packed their picnic baskets and began the long walk to the river. Gobo led the way, with Wembley at his side. They were headed for the Fraggles' favorite swimming hole, located at the bottom of a deep cavern. Red, Mokey, and the others were supposed to meet them there later. It was always a special day when the Fraggles went swimming in the river.

The river that runs through Fraggle Rock has a mind of its own. Sometimes it flows upstream. Sometimes it flows downstream. Other times it twists and turns so much, it forgets which way it was going, and ends up just sitting there in a pond.

The Fraggle Rock river has no beginning, and no Fraggle has ever seen its end. The river is sort of everywhere at once—flowing under a rock here, spilling into a waterfall there. You can never be sure where it might turn up. But ever since the first Fraggles ate Doozer sticks, a song has taught Fraggles about the river. Gobo, Wembley, and the others were singing that song as they walked along.

> " 'Come,' said the river. 'Come swim away with me.
> We'll go to far-off places that you'll be the first to see.
> You'll ride my rushing waters, past the Outer Maze
>   and more,
> But wave good-bye to all Fraggles, it's a one-way trip to
>   that distant shore.' "

Most Fraggles think that this is just another song. Actually, though, it teaches little Fraggles the dangers of the river. In the ponds and the pools, where the river bends, it's safe to swim. But where the water runs fast, a Fraggle can get swept away. And then it's the old one-way trip—a journey from which no Fraggle has ever returned.

"Not even for your birthday?" Wembley asked Gobo.

"No, you never return," Gobo told him. "Not even if you left your toothbrush behind."

Wembley stared at the river gurgling happily beside him. "Hey, Gobo," he said, "it looks sort of rough today, don't you think? Maybe we should climb the Curlicue Chimneys instead. We could have our picnic up on the plateau."

"The river is just water, Wembley," Gobo said. "There's nothing to be afraid of. Fraggles have always gone swimming in the river. As long as we stay in the lily-pad pools, it's safe. You just have to be careful, like the song says. You wouldn't jump in at the Doozer Helmet Rapids, would you?"

"Of course not!" Wembley cried. "Only a silly would swim there!"

The swimming hole that Gobo and Wembley were headed for was called Shoelace Swing Pond. Long ago some brave Fraggle had taken the shoelace from one of Pa Gorg's giant boots and tied it to a stalagmite that hung out over the pond. Ever since, Fraggles have been swinging from that shoelace and landing in the water.

The only problem is that the pond is small. Just around the bend trouble lurks. There the water roars between two ugly rocks that look just like giant Doozer helmets. Not surprisingly, this is called the Doozer Helmet Rapids. The rapids are not the best place for a lazy bath, although if you like bouncing off rocks at high speed, it is a lovely place to swim.

The long walk had made everyone hot and dusty. So when they finally got to the river, a whole gaggle of Fraggles headed for the water and began splashing about in the pond. Gobo tore off his vest, tossed it on top of a rock, and ran for the shoelace.

"Last one in is a cloudy Doozer stick!" he yelled, grabbing the lace. He flew high over the water, did a neat flip with a half-gainer, and fell into the pond with a splash. "Come on in, Wembley!" he called above the noise of the other swimming Fraggles.

Wembley didn't move. He was staring at the swing.

"Wembley, come on!" Gobo yelled louder. Wembley turned toward the pond. Slowly his eyes were drawn toward the thundering water at the Doozer Helmet Rapids. His mouth hung open.

Gobo swam back to shore and went to his roommate. "Hey, Wembley," he laughed. "If you keep that mouth open any longer, a rock clinger is going to build a nest in it."

"Ah . . . the pond's too shallow . . . ah . . . it's too crowded," Wembley said quickly. "Besides, I never . . . ah . . . get wet this soon after the Festival of the Bells."

"Wembley, trust me," said Gobo. "Fraggles have always gone swimming here."

"I know, I know," Wembley said.

"So what's up?" Gobo demanded.

Wembley looked down at his feet. "It's the song."

"The song?" Gobo asked. "What song?"

"You know. 'Come,' said the river. 'Come swim away with me.'" A shiver went through Wembley as he sang the words.

"Wembley, do you think the river wants to take you away?" Gobo asked.

Wembley nodded. "The river's different today. It's never been this fast before. Has it, Gobo?"

Gobo shook his head. "Wembley, the river hasn't changed," he said. "It's the same river Uncle Traveling Matt swam in. Every Fraggle ever born swam here. The song is just a song. Nothing's going to happen to you. Now, come on!"

Most of the other Fraggles in the water were staring at Wembley. By now any normal Fraggle would have grabbed the swing and splashed down in the water.

"Come on, Wembley! It's your turn," one Fraggle called from the distance.

"Honestly, Wembley," Gobo said encouragingly, "you'll be fine. You've gone swimming here a million times, haven't you?"

Wembley nodded.

Gobo handed him the rope. "So go ahead. Give it a try."

Wembley walked slowly to the edge. Ever so slowly he leaned out over the water. Then he just stood there.

"This rope looks a little frayed," he said.

"How about a push?" someone yelled. Suddenly a bunch of fun-loving Fraggles gave Wembley a shove in the back, and he swung high out over the pond.

"Let go!" Gobo yelled. But at that moment the shoelace snapped. Wembley kept right on swinging and landed with a big splash far outside the pond. The fast water began to nibble at his toes.

At first everyone laughed. But then Gobo started to get worried. Something was wrong. Like most of the Fraggles, Wembley was usually a good swimmer. But for some reason he wasn't swimming back to shore.

"Swim, Wembley, swim!" Gobo cried. But Wembley just bobbed along in the water. He was floating away.

Gobo turned and ran down the riverbank. He had to get ahead of Wembley and rescue him before Wembley reached the rapids. Gobo raced up the path that wound between the rocks. He was almost past Wembley when, coming around a bend, he stopped dead in his tracks. A huge boulder blocked the path.

Gobo turned toward the river. For the first time he could see why Wembley wasn't swimming. The shoelace was tangled around Wembley's legs, and he could barely move. Gobo watched helplessly as Wembley was sucked around the bend.

The old one-way trip had begun.

2

Found and Lost

IT only took Gobo a second to decide what to do when he saw Wembley disappear. He ran back to the swing, grabbed the picnic basket, threw it in the water, and flung himself on it. Then he paddled madly after his best friend.

It's all my fault, he thought frantically. *I made him jump. And even if Wembley can make it through the Doozer Helmet Rapids, then what? Where will the river take him? He still may never see Fraggle Rock again.* Gobo felt as terrible as he had ever felt in his life.

Some Fraggles have all the luck. The rest don't need any. Wembley was still hopelessly tangled in the shoelace when he passed between the Doozer Helmet rocks. But that was what saved him. As he floated past, the shoelace hooked on the rocks, stopping him. The current did the rest, pushing him over to the bank. There he climbed out of the shallow water and untied himself.

"Wait until Gobo sees me!" Wembley said proudly to himself. He began running back up the riverbank toward the shoelace swing. "That nasty river doesn't scare me anymore!"

But Gobo was having problems of his own. As he entered the rapids, he didn't see Wembley. He saw only rushing water and jagged rocks—and then stars. As he passed one of the Doozer Helmet boulders, the basket bounced up and his head hit a rock. The picnic basket floated on with Gobo aboard, out cold.

Gobo floated past the rapids and into calm water again. The river carried him through Fraggle Rock, but he saw none of it. Farther downstream he floated past Boober. Boober was doing a load of laundry. He saw Gobo and yelled a hello, but the great explorer seemed to be napping.

That's odd, thought Boober. *The river can be dangerous. Gobo shouldn't be sleeping.* He called out again, but Gobo didn't answer. Really worried now, Boober rinsed out the last of his towels and rags and went in search of Mokey, Red, and Wembley.

Meanwhile Gobo and the picnic basket floated onward. They drifted through many places Gobo had already explored, and some areas of the Rock he had never seen—places beyond the Outer Maze, places without names, places that even his Uncle Traveling Matt had never seen. If Gobo had been awake, he would have been able to fill in many empty areas on his maps. As it was, they stayed blank. Gobo slept on, and floated away.

By the time Wembley managed to climb over the boulder and make his way back to the Shoelace Swing Pond, most of the other Fraggles had run off to get help. The few that remained were scared out of their fur. They never expected to see Wembley again. So when he came back around the bend, they were terrified.

"It's a ghost!" someone screamed. And they ran away in all directions.

"Hey, it's me! I'm Wembley!" he shouted after them. "Where's Gobo? Isn't anyone glad to see me?"

Just then Red and Mokey came running down the shoreline. A group of Fraggles was close behind.

"See? There's Wembley!" Red cried when she caught sight of him. "I told you there was nothing to worry about." She stopped suddenly, and everyone else piled into her, almost knocking her down. "Relax! What's the hurry? I knew Gobo would take care of everything."

The Fraggles all cheered. Wembley was so glad to be safe and surrounded by the welcoming party he deserved that for the moment he forgot about Gobo.

The Fraggles picked Wembley up on their shoulders and carried him off, singing a new version of the river song:

" 'Come,' said the river. 'Come swim away with me.'
   Wembley fell in the water, but managed to get free!"

Mokey was the first to realize something was wrong.

"Where's Gobo?" she called above the noise of the celebration.

"Yeah, where *is* Gobo?" Wembley asked.

"Gobo's okay," Red said. "Wembley was the one who was lost!"

"But where could he be?" Wembley asked.

"Aw, he's probably just off exploring somewhere," Red said.

"He wouldn't just go off like that if Wembley was in danger," said Mokey, frowning. "And look!" She pointed at Gobo's vest, which was still hanging on the rock. "Gobo would never go exploring without his vest. He's always properly dressed."

"Maybe he was hot," Red said, starting to feel uneasy. "Or he got tired of wearing a vest. Or—"

One of the younger Fraggles tugged on Red's sweater. "Red," he said, "I saw Gobo. He was going after Wembley on top of his picnic basket."

At that moment Boober came around the corner at a trot. When he saw his friends, he stopped short. "Thank the Rock I found you," he gasped. "What's going on with Gobo?"

"You saw Gobo?" Red asked him.

"Yes. He just went past me. And—"

"See?" Red turned triumphantly to the others. "I told you he was all right. Did he say where he was going, Boober?"

"No, he was asleep. And that's just the—"

"Asleep?" Mokey said. Her voice sounded strange. "Where? When?"

"Downstream a bit, near Laughing Rock, just a few minutes ago," Boober stammered. "Why? I just know something

is wrong. My fur started itching the minute I saw him. And I
tried to—"

"What do you mean, asleep, Boober?" Mokey broke in.

Boober stamped his foot. "That's what I've been trying to
tell you! He was floating along on top of a picnic basket,
sleeping like a baby Fraggle. I thought it was pretty dangerous, being asleep on the river. So I yelled to him. But he
didn't wake up."

Red and Mokey looked at each other. Their fear was as
plain as the fur on their faces. Something was very wrong.

"Gobo could be floating in the Outer Maze by now," Red
said worriedly.

"We have to head him off!" Mokey cried. "Come on,
everybody. We have to save Gobo!"

Without another word, Fraggles started running after Red
and Mokey. If they didn't catch up with Gobo before he got
to the Outer Maze, there wasn't going to be any Gobo to
rescue.

Boober was left standing alone with Wembley, who was
too scared to move.

"Oh, Boober," Wembley moaned. "What are we going to
do?"

"I knew it! I just knew something like this would happen!"
Boober said. "Everybody always says I worry too much. But
see? Terrible things happen every day!"

"But we've got to try to save Gobo!" Wembley cried. "He's
my best friend, and he was trying to save *me*!"

"It's no use, Wembley." Boober shook his head. "Once the
river grabs you, it's over. You're a goner!"

"I won't believe that!" Wembley cried. "I have to try to do something!"

"Go ahead." Boober sighed. "I'll sit here and worry for both of us." He plopped down on a rock and sunk his head into his hands. "Maybe Gobo will float back this way."

Wembley ran off, not sure where he was going. He couldn't just sit there and do nothing. Boober wouldn't be the last Fraggle to tell Wembley that saving Gobo was going to be impossible. But Wembley wasn't going to give up yet.

3

Sad and Blue

FAR down the river, Gobo finally woke up. He saw absolutely nothing but dark purple-blue around him. The river was there beneath him, blue as always. But now everything else was blue, too.

"WEMBLEY!!" he shouted as loud as he could. But there was no answer, no echo. *Poor little guy,* he thought sadly. *I wonder where he is. I've never seen this part of the rock before, and I'm an explorer. Wembley won't have a chance unless I find him.*

Gobo kept floating, trying to figure out where he was. The shoreline stayed blue. *Boy, I wish I had my maps,* he thought. *I bet no other Fraggle has ever been this far down the river, not even my Uncle Matt!*

But floating around wasn't getting him anywhere. "Time to get going," he said out loud. He liked hearing the sound of his own voice, so he went on. "I guess I ought to paddle over to the shore and start looking for Wembley."

"Paddle over this way," a voice commanded out of the blueness.

Gobo almost fell off his picnic basket. Was that Red? The voice giggled the way Red giggles. "Red?" Gobo asked.

"I'm not red," the voice chuckled back. "I'm blue."

"Of course you're blue," Gobo snapped. "Everything's blue here. . . . But where are you? I can't see you."

"We Chortls know exactly where we are," the voice said. "You're the one who's lost!"

"Who says I'm lost? I'm searching for my friend Wembley."

"Well, he's not here," the Chortl said. "That's plain to see."

"Wembley is green," Gobo agreed sadly. "He would be plain to see in all this blue."

Gobo squinted. He could barely see the Chortl's body against the blue rocks. It looked like a beach ball with most of the air let out. Its skin was like Boober's famous zucchini hash, only blue. As it spoke, its body shook as if it were laughing. One long crease made up its broad, grinning mouth. Its eyes were nothing but twinkles.

"Gak!" Gobo yelped, stumbling onto the blue shore.

"Watch it!" the Chortl said. "Those are my toes you're gakking!"

"I've never seen anything like you!" Gobo exclaimed. "You talk in laughter and your toes are the size of my head."

"I've never seen anything like *you!*" it replied. "And I'd try to be polite if I were you. After all, *I'm* not the one who's lost."

"I told you, I'm not lost! I'm . . . an explorer!" Gobo tried to stand up taller.

"You look rather lost to me," the Chortl said.

"Well, I'm not," Gobo insisted. "I'm looking for my friend Wembley. *He's* the one who's lost."

"I see. Well, what would you do normally if you were . . . uh . . . lost?" the Chortl chuckled. "I wouldn't know. I'm never lost. Can't get lost around here. Everything's the same. Kind of blue."

"First, I'd sit down," Gobo said, plopping himself down against the Chortl's foot, which he sunk into like a pillow. "Then I'd follow my Uncle Traveling Matt's three rules for explorers who get lost—uh, who are exploring."

The Chortl gave a huge guffaw. "Oh, yes, indeedee do! Good idea! What's the first rule?"

" 'Remember the way you got in, so you can find your way out.' "

"Simple enough. How'd you get here?"

"That's a problem," Gobo had to admit. "I was knocked out and didn't see much."

"So what?" the Chortl said. "There are other senses, you know. Eyes aren't much good around here, anyway. I hardly use mine."

The Chortl blobbed over the river and flopped in. "Come on," it said. "Let me show you how to notice a few things around here. Things your eyes can't see." Gobo didn't have a whole lot to do, so he took the picnic basket and went along for the ride on the Chortl's back.

"Smell that?" the Chortl said as it floated along. "I'll bet the Harrumps have been hanging their squeemish out to dry." The Chortl's body shook with glee. "And feel those vibrations? The Lesser Leviathan has just taken another step. And the water here tastes funny. I'll bet the balders are in bloom!"

Gobo smelled the squeemish, felt the Leviathan's steps, and tasted the blooming balders. He noticed that not every rock looked quite so blue. Some were starting to look purple. Some were nearly black-green. And where the blue rock hummed, the river took a turn shaped like a Fraggle's tail.

"I won't forget that the next time I come through this way," Gobo told himself. "But which way is this way?"

The Chortl took Gobo to the very edge of the blueness. There the river flowed straight up, like an upside-down waterfall. It was higher than a couple of Gorgs standing on each other's shoulders. Then the water turned in midair and poured sideways, disappearing off the blue edge of the Chortl's world.

"Last stop! End of the line," the Chortl was giggling. "I get confused past here. The river up there has too many colors for me."

For a moment Gobo felt frightened. *Where was he headed?* he wondered. But then he remembered that he was looking for Wembley. He squared his shoulders.

"Well, thanks for the ride," he said, not finding any hand, paw, or fin on the Chortl to shake. "See you sometime, I guess."

"No, you won't," the Chortl replied with a big ha-ha-ha. "Sense me. Don't see me."

Gobo let himself be carried straight up the upside-down waterfall. He looked down at the blue Chortl, who was quickly disappearing against the blue world. And although Gobo couldn't see him, he could smell that the Chortl would miss him.

4

Black, Black, Black, Black, Black

The upside-down waterfall brought Gobo to a land wild with colors. They were so bright that his eyes hurt. There were trees with leaves that were all the colors of the rainbow. There were pink rocks and orange bushes. Strange creatures with phosphorescent stripes, luminescent dots, and sparklescent fur ran along the brilliant shoreline.

"What kind of place is this?" Gobo wondered out loud. "It looks like Mokey painted everything backwards."

"How would you know?" a voice answered. "You're mostly one color, and a dull orange at that!"

Gobo turned to see a purple face with lime eyes that stared out at him. "My tail is purple, I'll have you know," he corrected the head.

"Only two colors! Ugh! How boring!" said a creature with an aqua head, turning up its nose.

Gobo paddled over to the bronze shore. That's when he realized that both heads actually belonged to the same body. In fact Gobo counted six heads in all. Each was a different color, and each sat on a long neck that bobbed about in every direction. A thousand feet ran under the beast.

"Oooooh! He's got only one head!" cried the fuchsia head.

"And two tiny feet!" a puce head added.

"Excuse me," Gobo interrupted. "I'm looking for my friend Wembley. Perhaps one of you heads saw him?"

"Black, black, black, black . . ." the heads all began saying at once. At the same time the thousand feet ran in a thousand different directions. The body was pulled left and right. Then it went round and round until it fell down.

"Why are you all saying black?" Gobo asked.

"Black means we disagree," the purple head replied. Quickly it was yanked off toward a flower. Three of the others seemed to be hungry, because they started gobbling what looked like billions of bits of shattered scarlet crystals. "It also means you're full of fuzz," the puce head added, "and nozschmozkapop! We never disagree politely if we can help it."

"Well, all your heads don't seem much better than one to me," Gobo said. "You can't decide which way to go. And I can see why Uncle Matt's second rule wouldn't work here."

"Why not?" the fuchsia head demanded. "And what's a rule?"

"Matt says I'm supposed to head for a goal. But every-

thing's too colorful here. Nothing stands out like a goal should. It's as bad as the all-blue world!"

"Follow me!" The fuchsia head beckoned to Gobo.

"No, me!" a chartreuse one pleaded.

"Black, black, black, black!!!" the assembled heads cried as the beast galloped off in a mess of directions.

Gobo got back on his picnic basket and floated away. "I guess I'll have to forget Uncle Matt's second rule," he decided. "I just hope Wembley keeps swimming. Or else . . ."

Gobo didn't want to think about that.

Wembley cheered up considerably when he arrived at the Great Hall.

Red was standing on top of a large rock, organizing the search parties for Gobo. "Head for the Outer Maze! Run for the Spiral Cavern! Wembley, sound the alarm!" she cried, dancing around on top of the rock. Wembley sat down on the cave floor, howling his fire siren as loud as he could, while Fraggles ran around in all directions.

Fraggles were all over the place. Everyone wanted to help. Fraggles bonked into one another. Fraggles stepped on tails. Some ran in circles, and others just started running because everyone else was running. In the center, Red kept barking orders.

"Collect some grapevines for ropes. Put a watch on the bridges. Search the dead-end tunnels. Hurry! Hurry! Hurry! Every second counts!"

After a few minutes the Great Hall was just about empty. Red and Mokey came over and helped Wembley to his feet.

He was covered with dust and the footprints of a thousand confused Fraggles.

"This is all my fault," Wembley moaned. "Gobo was trying to help me."

"Don't worry, Wembley!" Red commanded. "There are a thousand Fraggles out there looking for Gobo. We'll find him before he floats out of Fraggle Rock. That river flows through just about every tunnel and cave in the Rock. Gobo's got to be in one of them, or my name isn't Red Fraggle."

"Isn't there anything else we can do?" Wembley asked sadly. "We can't just sit here and wait."

"We don't have time to wait." Mokey put her hand on Red's arm. She looked worried. "I've been thinking. The river moves so fast that Gobo could be beyond the Outer Maze before any of those search parties find him. There's got to be a better way to do this!"

Wembley leaped into the air. "The maps! Gobo's maps will help!"

"Who cares about some stupid maps?" Red complained.

But Mokey and Wembley were already running for Gobo's cave. One whole wall was covered with yellowed maps and charts of all the tunnels and caves in Fraggle Rock. Gobo's Uncle Traveling Matt, the great explorer, had made them long ago. Gobo himself had filled in many of the blank areas.

Mokey spread out the map marked "Beyond the Outer Maze and More" and studied it.

"Look! There's a place where the river pours right into a hole in the rock!" she said, pointing at the map. "Gobo called it the Gullet. It's so small, Gobo and that picnic

basket would never fit through. He could be stuck there, floating around in this pond!"

Wembley jumped up and down. "Gobo showed it to me once! He's safe! Yippee!"

"Wait a minute." Red had come up quietly behind them and was now looking over their shoulders at the map. "There's a good chance he would never have floated that way. See? There's a fork in the river farther upstream." She pointed to a spot where the line split apart. "The current might have taken him this way. And that would send him to . . ." Red had to stare hard at the tiny letters on the old map. "It's called STO PGOBA CKDAN GER."

"What a goofy name!" Wembley exclaimed.

Mokey looked closely at the map. "Wait." She read it slowly. "Stop . . . go . . . back . . . danger."

"Rotten radishes," Red grumbled.

"We'd better hurry," Wembley cried, running out the door. But Red and Mokey didn't bother to follow. "C'mon, you guys!" Wembley said, sticking his head back inside.

Red and Mokey just stood there, staring at him. They both looked very strange.

"Go where?" Mokey asked him, staring at the vast empty space on the map. "There's nowhere to go. Gobo's out here somewhere. But there's no way any of us is going to find him. We just have to hope that he makes it back here somehow."

Wembley looked at Mokey and Red. "But we can't just . . ."

Mokey shook her head. She reached out and took Wembley's hand. "Don't you see, Wembley?" she said, with a catch in her throat. "It's no use."

"What's no use?" Wembley cried. "We've got to save Gobo! Red?"

But Red just stared down at the floor.

Mokey began to cry first. Then Red broke down, too. "This is awful," she sobbed. "Just awful. Gobo's gone!"

Wembley felt his own eyes fill with tears. *Brave Fraggles don't cry!* he thought angrily to himself. *That's what Gobo always says.* And then he realized he would never hear Gobo say anything again.

That was when Wembley started to have a funny feeling. It was like an itch deep inside. He tried to ignore it, but the sadder he became, the more he felt it. It started in his toes and stretched all the way to his nose. There seemed to be no way to scratch it.

Then Wembley became very angry. His stomach locked. Words jumped out of his mouth. "Hold it!" he bellowed. "We can't give up. This is Gobo! Our friend! We have to do *something*!"

Mokey and Red looked at him as if he were a little crazy. "Wembley," Mokey began, "there's nothing we *can* do."

"Don't say that," Wembley cried. "Gobo would never give up on a friend in trouble!" He turned away from them and began walking back toward the Great Hall.

"Wembley, wait!" Red shouted.

But Wembley kept marching. He wasn't quite sure what he was going to do, but he was going to do something. That itch had to be scratched. It was the itch some call courage.

5

No Fraggle Is an Island

GOBO was starting to get scared. He was more lost than he had ever been. He had traveled too far by now to walk back . . . even if he knew which way to go. He still hadn't found Wembley, and nothing up ahead looked anything like Fraggle Rock. To fight off panic, Gobo turned to Uncle Matt's third rule for explorers. "Don't keep going when you're lost," it went. "Wait for help."

That seemed like a good idea. If he really was lost, why get more lost? So Gobo paddled over to a small island to wait. The island was the color Mokey gets when she's not feeling well.

Gobo opened his basket. He found a few soggy radish sandwiches and some Doozer sticks.

Following the third rule might not be such a good idea, he thought. *This food is going to run out soon. And I could be here forever. . . .* He started to feel panicky. "Wembley," he cried. "Where are you? And where am I?"

"You're right here! And uninvited, I might add!"

Gobo was startled almost out of his fur. He dropped the rest of his dessert into a deep hole in front of him.

"Not bad," the hole said. "But next time try a dash of balder on that. And watch where you put your feet, mister! That's my face!"

Gobo jumped up. "Who's talking?" he cried.

"Me. The island," the hole replied. "And you're still on my face."

Gobo stepped toward the shore. "It's not my fault," he said. "I don't know where to stand. Anyway, I might as well leave. I'm not getting anywhere staying here." And he started climbing back on board his picnic basket.

"Naw, c'mon, don't leave!" the island cried. "Being an island gets a little lonely. No one has stopped here since I was just a stepping-stone."

"Well . . ." Gobo stepped back away from the basket. "I'm sort of looking for my friend Wembley. You haven't seen him go by, have you?"

"A lot of stuff floats by here," the island said. "But none of it ever called itself Wembley."

"He's short, green, and wears brightly colored shirts," Gobo said.

"We got too many bright colors around here already, son," the island sighed. "But if this Wembley looks anything like you, I haven't seen him."

"My friends say we look a bit alike," Gobo said. He

thought of Red, Mokey, Boober, and Wembley, and his eyes filled with tears. "I miss them," he said, his voice cracking. "And I miss my home."

Gobo hung his head. As he looked down, he noticed two puddles. They were near the hole, and they were getting bigger. The island was crying!

"I wish I could be lost," it sniffed. "If only I could wander off a few miles. I'd love to get away from this same old scenery. At least you can leave. I'm stuck here."

"I can't leave. Uncle Matt's rule says I have to wait for help."

"Bah! Not every rule fits every situation!" the island yelled. The hole opened so large that Gobo almost fell in.

"But Uncle Matt's the greatest explor—"

"Listen, son, I can't say I've been around. After all, I've been an island all my life. I always wanted to be a raft. Or maybe a flying creature. Wings would look good on me. . . . But anyway, I've learned a lot just sitting here. And I can tell you one thing. Rules don't always work in life. Sometimes you have to trust your own instincts. I think it's about time for another rule. How about: 'Sometimes you have to break all the old rules'?" He gave Gobo a whack on the back with a golden palm tree. "Besides, you can't get any more lost!"

Gobo looked downstream. "I guess you're right. I just have to keep on going. Uncle Matt's third rule has to be wrong this time." He climbed aboard his picnic basket once again. "I wonder what's at the end of the river."

"What makes you think there is an end?" the island called

after Gobo as he disappeared around the bend. But Gobo didn't have an answer.

One by one, dejected Fraggles drifted back to the Great Hall. None of them had found Gobo. Indeed, it was becoming clear that he might never be found.

Finally, everyone was there but Wembley. No one could find him either. A thousand Fraggles looked to Gobo's friends—Mokey, Red, and Boober—for comfort. They waited for Wembley for a while longer. But finally, Mokey climbed the big rock and raised her hands for silence.

"Gobo is gone," she said simply. "And nothing that I say is going to make any of us feel any better. But let us hope that he hasn't given up. Gobo is a great explorer. Maybe, somehow, he will find his way home to us."

None of the Fraggles moved. No one spoke. The Great Hall was silent with grief.

Mokey's words echoed back across the bowed heads. "I tried to write a poem for Gobo, but I was too sad to finish it. Every line ended in *distant shore*, and the only rhyme I could think of was *nevermore*." Mokey found it hard to speak. Red tried to help her down off the big rock, but Mokey wasn't through.

"As long as brave Fraggles wonder why,
There will be other Gobos ready to try . . ."

Mokey turned away, unable to continue.

Red climbed up next to speak to the crowd. "I know we're all sorry about Gobo. But we have to listen to Mokey, and keep hoping." Red blinked back a tear. "I love Gobo and I know you do, too. And Gobo is the greatest explorer Fraggle Rock has ever known. I have faith in him," she continued. "If anyone can find his way back to Fraggle Rock, Gobo can!"

Boober was next. He felt pretty uncomfortable in front of all those Fraggles, but he had an important message to deliver. He closed his eyes, pretending there was no one else out there, and started to speak. "A lot of you think I'm always too pessimistic, always expecting the worst to happen," Boober mumbled into his scarf.

A few voices in the back shouted, "Louder!"

"But this proves my point. The river song warned us. Gobo knew he was taking a risk trying to save Wembley. That's what friends do. But we should all be more careful to begin with. So please, sing the river song all the time. Listen to the words. And stay away from the rushing waters! We owe it to Gobo!"

The Great Hall was silent. Then a few of the Fraggles began to sing the river song. Soon everyone was singing together.

The music flowed down the tunnels and echoed into the deepest corners of the Rock. It found Wembley alongside the river. He had another picnic basket packed beside him.

But when Wembley heard the words "Wave good-bye to all Fraggles," Wembley knew he couldn't leave them all just yet. He had something to tell them.

He picked up his picnic basket and ran back to the Great Hall. They waited in silence as he climbed the rock.

"Gobo was my best friend. We did everything together," he began. "I have decided that I don't want to be here if Gobo's not here." Wembley drew himself up to his full height, which wasn't that high to begin with. "I'm going to let myself be carried away by the river. At least then I'll be with Gobo. I'm going to jump in that river. And I'm going to take my picnic basket with me. And maybe, just maybe, me and Gobo, someday, we'll have a picnic together on that distant shore."

Wembley held his chin up and fought off the tears. He had to be brave for Gobo, he told himself. Then he climbed down off the rock and marched straight out of the Great Hall. None of the Fraggles even tried to stop him. They were too moved.

Wembley headed for the river.

6

Gobo's Fourth Rule

On another part of the river Gobo floated along, eating the last Doozer-stick crumbs from the bottom of the picnic basket. There was still no end to the river in sight.

I guess I'm headed for that distant shore, like the song says, he thought. *But I just know it will never be as much fun there as it was in Fraggle Rock. I wish Wembley were here. And Red and Boober and Mokey, too. I wish all the Fraggles were coming along with me.*

Unfortunately Gobo would have to take his last voyage alone. Even the strange creatures on the riverbank had disappeared. The land of colors faded into black and white. A land of spikes came next. That was followed by mists and fogs that were good to eat—luckily for Gobo, since the picnic basket was now empty. All he had to do was open his mouth for a meal.

At times the river became very shallow. Once it disappeared into a trickle, and Gobo had to walk. He went through tunnels that had only one end. Bridges made from beautifully carved stone stretched above him. All along the bank stood crystal ruins. They looked like castles, but no one lived in them.

Farther down the river, Gobo came upon square boxes floating in the water. Each was soft and covered with furry foam. Then the river got lumpy and thick. Great winds howled. Sheer cliffs rose on either side of Gobo.

And finally there was only the water. The shoreline disappeared. As far as Gobo could see, there was nothing but wide, blue, boring water. The river seemed to go on and on forever.

I can't give up, Gobo thought. *If I do, I'm really done for. And so is Wembley.* But it was hard to keep his spirits up. Things looked pretty hopeless.

Gobo felt sadder than ten of the days Boober got out on the wrong side of his bed. He felt more lonely than a hundred Uncle Traveling Matts alone in Outer Space. Even a Gorg would have looked good right then. At least Gorgs were part of Fraggle Rock.

"I wish I were home," Gobo sighed, and closed his eyes. A single tear dripped off his nose. It sent out a circular wave of ripples in the river.

New ripples came back across the calm water. When they touched the spot where his tear had landed, he heard words.

"Gobo, you are home. You never left," the river gurgled. "When you ride me, the scenery changes. But the river is still the same."

"I don't understand," Gobo said. "Who are you?"

"Water is water," the river replied. "Rivers are rivers. Fraggles are Fraggles. They go, they come. It's all the same. Now we start all over again."

With that, the water began spinning as if someone had pulled a giant plug. The spinning grew faster. Gobo hung on to the picnic basket. Then a tunnel of water opened up in the center of the whirlpool. Gobo kept his eyes closed, and held his nose. Down he went.

When Gobo opened his eyes again, he was still on the river. The picnic basket was beneath him. But the shoreline looked strangely familiar. Wasn't that Doozer Bridge Corners up ahead? And Gobo recognized a rock shaped like the Trash Heap. The green ball of fur standing there holding a picnic basket looked familiar, too.

"Wembley!" Gobo cried.

"Oh, hi, Gobo," Wembley mumbled, looking up. Then he jumped straight up into the air. "Gobo! You came back! Is that really you?"

"Of course it's me!" Gobo answered, paddling over to the side. "I finally found you!"

"But I was never lost!" Wembley tried to explain. "You were the one who got swept away."

"Who, me?" Gobo said. "I never get lost! I'm an explorer, and I always follow the rules. . . ."

Gobo's voice died away. He stood there for a moment, thinking.

"I *was* lost, Wembley," he finally admitted, taking his friend's hand. "None of the rules worked. But I learned an important lesson. Fraggles make up rules because they seem to help. Sometimes they don't. But that's when you have to keep going anyway—even when it makes no sense."

The two friends hugged each other on the riverbank. Then they started to walk toward the Great Hall.

"What happened to you, Gobo?" Wembley asked as they walked.

Gobo wanted to tell Wembley about all the places he had been and the creatures he had met. But he didn't know where to start. For that matter, now that he was back in Fraggle Rock, Gobo wasn't at all sure of what had really happened. The Chortl and the island and the talking river all seemed like a strange dream.

So he just smiled and patted Wembley on the back. "I'll tell you all about it someday," he promised.

"I know!" Wembley said, stopping suddenly. "We can go on our picnic after all, and you can tell me then! Can we, Gobo?"

Gobo held up the empty picnic basket. "I think I ate our picnic, Wembley," he laughed.

Then Gobo noticed Wembley's full picnic basket. "Hey, Wembley, what's that basket for?" he asked.

Wembley hung his head. "I was just about to toss it into the river and go after you," he admitted. "I didn't care if I never came back."

Gobo gave him another hug. "Thanks, Wembley. And I thought I was the one trying to save *you!*"

"You did, Gobo! Honest, you did."

"Hey, where are Red and Boober and Mokey?" Gobo asked. "They can join our picnic!"

"I'll go get them!" Wembley cried happily.

He ran off toward the Great Hall at top speed, howling with joy.

Gobo smiled. And behind him the river kept rolling on by, heading for home.